First published in this collection in 1989
by Methuen Children's Books
a Division of the Octopus Publishing Group
Michelin House, 81 Fulham Road, London SW3 6RB
Stories by Peter Bonnici
Pictures by Lisa Kopper
From an original idea by Shirley-Anne Lewis
Licensed by Link Licensing Ltd
Copyright © 1988 Barney Entertainments Ltd
Acknowledgement: Backgrounds, Isabel Pearce
ISBN 0416 152422
Printed in Great Britain by Scotprint, Musselburgh

BARNEY'S
Big Book of Stories

Stories by Peter Bonnici
Pictures by Lisa Kopper
From an original idea by Shirley-Anne Lewis

Methuen Children's Books

BARNEY'S
Treasure Hunt

Spring had come at last.
Barney bounced into the garden,
full of life. "Time to romp about
in the grass," he said.

Roger the mouse was still sleepy
after a long winter in his snug home
in Barney's fur. "This sounds too much
like hard work," he thought, "I'm off."

Carefully, ever so quietly, Roger climbed down
from his bedroom on Barney's head and started
to tip-toe back towards the warm house, but his
plan was ruined by a high voice...

"Ro-ger! Yoo-hoo, Roger!" It was Cornelia,
all dressed up for gardening. She waved a pink
trowel.

Roger sat beside the garden gnome and sulked.
There was no escape now – not even for Barney.

"I've got everything we need for gardening," said Cornelia.

Roger and Barney peered into the big box full of seed packets. There were lettuce seeds, spinach seeds, runner-bean seeds...

"There doesn't seem to be anything I like," growled Barney.

"Spinach is good for you," said Cornelia.

"But I like ice-cream," said Barney.

"Don't be silly," said Cornelia, "If you plant ice cream, it will melt when the sun comes out."

While Barney and Cornelia were fighting over
the seeds, Roger continued to search around in
the box. Suddenly he gave a loud squeak of
delight. He snatched up a couple of seed packets
and dashed off to a shady corner of the garden.

Barney shrugged, "Roger is
losing his marbles," he said.
"Sleeps too much in winter,
you know."

Cornelia returned to her garden to plant flowers. Barney decided to cut the grass.

"Must be sure everything works," he said as he plugged in the lawn mower.

He flicked the switch and the lawn mower burst into life. It was so powerful that Barney was dragged all over the garden. The grass cuttings sprayed up behind him, making him look like a mad skier in green snow.

Suddenly there was a loud CLUNK! The lawn mower spluttered to a stop.

"You've run over the garden gnome," said Cornelia, "and broken it."

"Oh, never mind," said Barney. "I'll try the hose now. Let's see if THAT still works."

He dumped the lawn mower under the apple tree and rushed to the tap under the kitchen window.

From inside the house came excited little noises from Roger. He was behaving in a most secretive way.

"What's that you've got there?" Barney called out.

"None of your business," said Roger. "It's mine – all mine," and he gave a wild little laugh.

But Barney ignored him – he was too busy testing the hose.

He turned on the tap. The hose sprang into life.
A loud shriek came from Cornelia's garden.
Barney turned to see what was going on and
found that the hose was spurting out water from
hundreds of holes in it.
Silly Barney! He'd mowed the hose
when he mowed the lawn.
Cornelia stood there dripping.
"You've ruined my hat!"
she wailed.

Barney scrambled around in the garden shed and
finally emerged with a battered straw hat.

"Take this," he said to Cornelia.

She took one look at the hat and wailed, "How
absolutely dreadful!" Barney tried to hide his
laugh when she put it on. She looked like a tiny
scarecrow.

"Back to work," said Barney. And back to work they went. Roger was still behaving most strangely. He had put an umbrella in the corner of the garden and was doing his secret work behind it.

Barney started to dig. Suddenly his spade hit
something hard. **CLUNK!**

"You've found a treasure chest!" yapped Cornelia.

Even Roger left his secret project and climbed onto Barney's head to see what he'd found.

Slowly, ever so carefully, Barney scraped away the soil and there, staring up at them was the most enormous marrow bone.

"TREASURE!" yelled Barney
and began to dig another hole
in the middle of the lawn. Roger was
not impressed. He slid down Barney's tail and
scurried off back to his secret corner. Cornelia
returned to her flowers.

After a few minutes digging Barney gave up
his second hole and started searching for treasure
in another place. And then another, and another.
But he just couldn't find any more.

By lunch time the garden looked a real mess. The broken lawn mower lay under the apple tree. The broken gnome had been shoved into the flower bed. The hose was still squirting water over everything. The lawn was now covered with dozens of deep holes, with piles of mud beside them.

And there, exhausted in the middle of all this, lay Barney. And there was still no treasure.

Roger climbed
onto Barney's tummy.
"If you had any sense," he said, "you
wouldn't have planted marrow bone seeds!"
Then he led Barney by the hand to his secret
corner of the garden. "I've planted seeds for all
my summer food," he announced proudly.

And there, stretching before him, Barney saw neat little rows of seed hills – each with a beautiful label:

CHEESEPLANT.

THE DAILY DOG

OGS MARCH FOR BONES

SNAPWORD

CROSSDOG

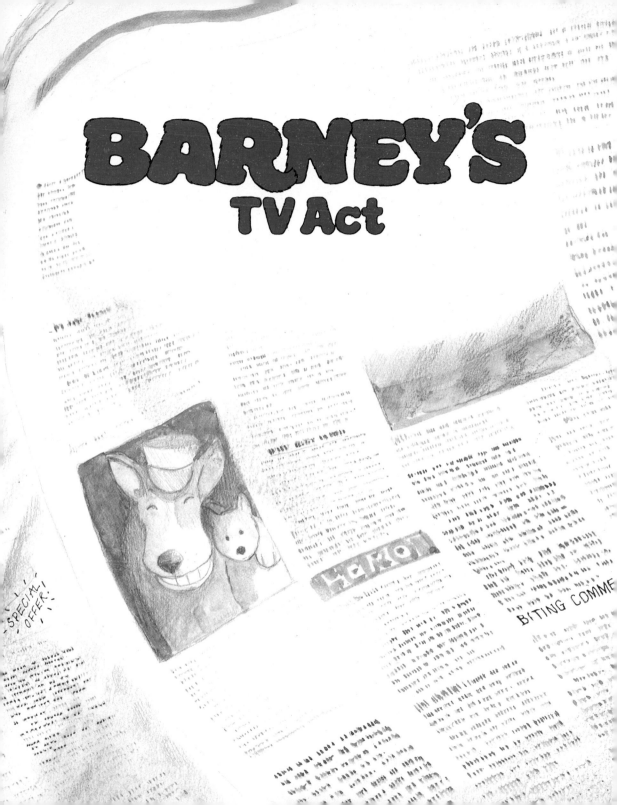

Every Tuesday at breakfast Barney enjoyed reading the paper. Roger the mouse peered out of his snug bedroom on top of Barney's head and squeaked with excitement.

"Look Barney, 'Good-Looking Dog Needed for New Television Show. Auditions Today!' That's you, my boy!"

In fact Roger got so excited that he lost his
balance and fell, splash, head first into Barney's
breakfast bowl. Barney fished Roger out with his
spoon. His eyes widened in amazement. "Do you
really think I can become a star?" he said.

"Certainly!" said Roger. "Even Cornelia the
Chihuahua says how clever you are at juggling
marrow bones."

"You're right," shouted Barney,
flinging his newspaper into the air
and knocking over his glass of milk.
He sprang across to the mirror.
"Oh you great, big, wonderful star,"
he said. "Now let's get out there and show the
world how amazing you are."

He gave himself a
quick lick and a brush,
grabbed his favourite dog collar
and was off!
   Poor Roger had a hard time catching up
on his tiny little feet. In fact he didn't
even have time to sniff at the cheese shop
as they hurried past on their way to the station.

"We'll need one and a half tickets to Glitter Town," said Barney.

"Where?" asked Roger, who was still out of breath as he struggled to climb back onto Barney's head.

Barney let out a deep sigh. "The place where stars are made, of course," he said. "We only need singles, because we'll be returning in a silver Rolls Royce."

TICKETS

The train pulled into the station.
On they clambered. The whistle blew.
The engine let out a long **H-O-O-T**
and chuffed off in a hiss of steam.

Soon trees and houses and fields were flashing
by, but all Barney could hear was the sound of
the wheels going: *YOU'RE-A-STAR;*

    YOU'RE-A-STAR;
     YOU'RE-A-STAR;
      YOU'RE-A-STAR.

Finally they arrived.
Television House was a huge
glass place with fancy cars
parked outside.
Barney and Roger were ushered
into the make-up room.
"I'm sure this place is full of
famous stars," whispered Barney
when they were alone. "Look there!" he pointed.
"And there!" he said.
"And there!" In fact, Barney thought
that everyone in Television House
was a star.

He was shoved down into a chair in front of a huge mirror with lights around it.

"All this hair, lovie," said the make-up assistant, "What can we do with it?"

"Nothing fancy, please," said Roger who was worried. After all, his bedroom was in Barney's head and he didn't want it all brushed out.

"As you like, sweetheart," said the make-up assistant. She clipped Barney's toenails and brushed his coat with a big stiff brush and ended by slapping hair oil all over to give him a wonderful shine.

The big moment had arrived.
Roger climbed back into Barney's
head. It was all sticky and slippery
with hair oil.

"Now, do everything I tell you," he
whispered to Barney. "And don't try to
show off."

Barney's name was called. Off he trotted onto
the studio floor with his marrow bones.

"Lights!" shouted the director. A strong spotlight shone on Barney.

"Music!" called the director. The piano player started a tune.

"Juggle," whispered Roger. And Barney juggled.

Everyone clapped.

"Now for your song," whispered Roger. And
Barney began to sing; but quite soon started to
jump around and dance a wild show-off dance.
    Roger yelled, "Stop! I can't hold on any longer!
The hair oil is too slippery."
    But Barney continued to twirl round and
round.

"Help!" yelled Roger as he lost his grip
and flew off Barney's head. Up, up, up he
flew. He swung from the lights. He slid
down the curtains. He bounced onto
Barney's head and with a double
somersault in the air landed **CRASH**
onto the camera.

Everyone cheered.

Barney thought the cheers were for him and gave a loud howl and jumped high into the air. Down he came with a thump, sliding across the studio floor, dragging down the curtains and props, crashing into the piano and ending up squashing the director under him.

"Out!" yelled the director.

"Out! Out! Out!"

EXIT

All was not lost, however. The director thought that Roger was a great acrobat and looked absolutely wonderful on the T.V. monitor. There and then he signed him up for a big part in the show!

So they did return home in a silver Rolls
Royce after all – but it was Roger and not
Barney sitting in the back.

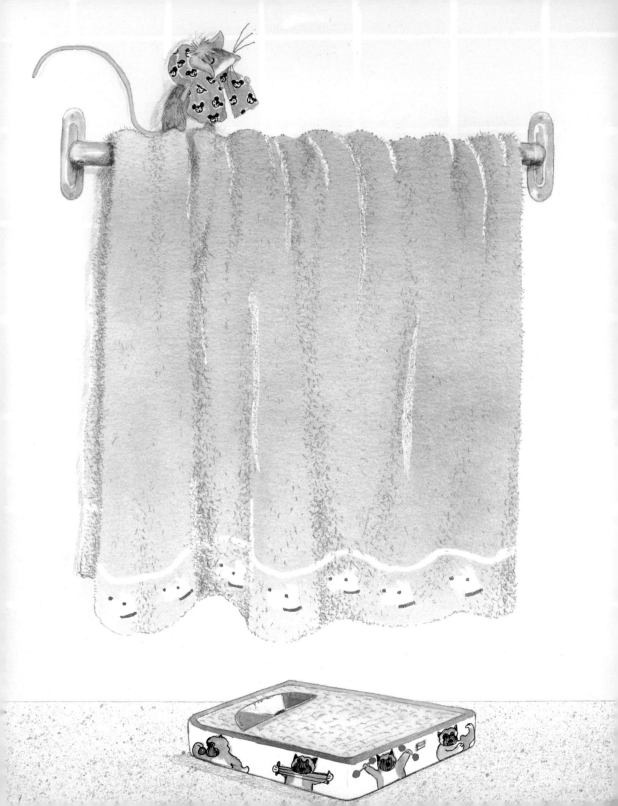

BARNEY'S
Hungry Day

Barney took one look at the bathroom
scales and let out a loud howl. Roger, who
was brushing his teeth, half in a dream,
was so startled that he fell into the
washbasin.

"Okay," he said, "now that you've finally managed to wake me, would you please explain what that was all about."

"I'm getting fat," wailed Barney. "Cornelia's always saying so, and now even the scales agree with her."

Roger leaned deep into the sponge and sighed.

At breakfast Roger knew that things were quite serious because instead of his usual helping, Barney just had a small glass of orange juice. Roger, of course, was quite happy to tuck into his bowl of cereal, followed by four slices of toast and a hunk of cheese.

And when Barney said, "I've got to start doing something about this weight," Roger knew things had got very serious indeed.

By the time Cornelia and Desmond the Afghan popped in for a visit, Barney looked a most sorry sight, slumped in his armchair.

Desmond prodded Barney in the tummy. "Nothing that can't be cured by a bit of exercise," he said.

When Barney didn't argue, Roger knew that things had become very, very serious.

"Of course you're right," said Barney. "I think I'll take a walk down to the shops, then."

"Walk?" said Desmond. "You're going to need more than that, old son."

Barney became quite pale. "Surely you don't expect me to run," he pleaded.

Desmond nodded and shoved Barney out of the house.

Barney jogged down the hill towards the greengrocer's where Mr Prophet was about to place the last orange on top of his beautiful pyramid.

"Can't be fat," huffed Barney. "Must lose weight," puffed Barney.

Mr Prophet watched in horror as Barney approached.

Like a runaway train, Barney charged past.
"Morning Proffffit," he puffed, knocking poor
Mr Prophet backwards into his neat pile of
oranges.

   "I knew he'd do it," said the Prophet of Doom
in his most serious voice as he rolled down the hill
like a log on a sunset river of oranges.

He turned and twisted slowly all the way down, finally coming to rest against a lamp-post. He noticed Barney in the distance turn off the road and enter the park.

BARKING PA

Mr Prophet carefully steadied himself against the lamp-post as he stood up. He picked the orange pips from his coat and glanced up to see if anybody had noticed his accident. There, charging down the hill, came Roger followed by Cornelia and Desmond.

"Stop, Barney!" yelled Roger. "Yoo hoo, Barney!" called Cornelia. "Watch out!" shouted Desmond. Too late...

..... They reached the scattered oranges and soon all three of them came tumbling down the hill. Mr Prophet held on to the lamp-post for safety and patiently watched Roger, Cornelia and Desmond roll screaming past him.

"Some people find strange ways of having fun," muttered Mr Prophet.

Roger and Cornelia were first into the park with Desmond trailing far behind. It was quite simple to see which way Barney had gone – he'd left a trail of clues. Flower beds had been trampled, a young puppy had been knocked into the pond with his sailing boat, ducks were scattered all over the place, then the trail led back home.

Out of breath, the three friends finally staggered into the living room only to find Barney glowing with good health.

He took one look at them and said, "You three should take up jogging, you know. It does wonders for you." Desmond flopped down onto the floor, rolled over onto his back and groaned.

When Roger had finally got his breath back he climbed back into his home on the top of Barney's head. He leaned over to Barney's right ear, lifted it and shouted: "WHY DIDN'T YOU STOP WHEN WE CALLED OUT TO YOU?"

Barney had that innocent look in his eye. "I was only trying to lose weight," he said.

"FOLLOW ME!" yelled Roger and he led
Barney out of the room, taking care to step
around Desmond as he did so. He pointed to the
bathroom scales. The needle was stuck on the red
section marked FAT.

Barney tapped it, but the needle didn't move.
He thumped on the scale but the needle still didn't
move. He jumped up and down on the scales but
the needle still didn't move.

Barney let out a loud howl: "Yippee! I'm not fat after all!" He charged past Roger, down the stairs, into the kitchen and helped himself to the most enormous plate of cake and biscuits you have ever seen. Yummy!

BARNEY'S
Christmas Surprise

Just as Roger was about to put the star on top of the Christmas tree there was a loud booming knock on the door.

It gave Barney such a fright that he let go of the wobbly ladder and dashed to the window to see who it was. The ladder crashed to the ground leaving Roger swinging from the star.

"Oh, it's only Mr Prophet," said Barney as he opened the door to a gloomy-eyed spaniel.

"Happy Christmas, old chap," said Barney in his most cheerful voice.

Mr Prophet just pushed past him with a grunt.

"Cold doorsteps are not the place to talk about Christmas," said Mr Prophet. "Christmas Eve is too early to decide whether it's happy or not." He whipped out a giant box of tissues and blew his nose with a large honking sound.
No wonder he was called
the Prophet of Doom.

He took one look at Roger swinging from the star
and said in his most miserable voice, "Don't think
much of your fairy."

"Get me down!" yelled Roger.

"So, it's a talking fairy," mumbled Mr Prophet.
He honked into his tissue again.
"Whatever will they think of next."

Barney helped Roger down from the tree,
sending a shower of pine needles all over
their visitor.

"Clumsy oaf," growled Mr Prophet,
shaking his coat wildly.

Barney and Roger backed towards the
door. "It must surely be time for mince
pies and tea," whispered Barney.

When they returned
with a tray piled high
with mince pies, they were most
surprised to find Mr Prophet crawling among the
beautifully wrapped presents under the tree.
"Can't see one with my name on it,"
he complained.

Barney gave Roger a quick look and then gave a little Barney cough. "Ahem!" he said. "Prophet is going to get a special surprise, isn't he Roger?"

But Roger was too busy with his nose deep in a mince pie. There was cream all over his face – it even blocked his ears.

"Humph!" said the Prophet of Doom, "I'll be back tomorrow, then," and he left. The house became quiet and peaceful once more.

Barney slumped back into his chair and sighed, "I do love Christmas," he said, "even if I have to spend every evening sweeping up pine needles."

Roger munched into his sixth mince pie. "So what's this special present for old Gloomy Doomy?" he asked, as he polished off the last of the cream.

"Something's bound to turn up," said Barney.

And no sooner had he spoken than there came a
soft tap on the door followed by the sweet sound
of carol singers. There, standing on the doorstep,
were two tiny dalmatian puppies. One had a
lamp over her shoulder.

"Where's the rest of the gang?" asked Barney.

"There's only us," said the puppies. "We don't really have anyone or anywhere to go."

"Can't have little things like you alone at Christmas," said Barney, and an idea came into his head. He swept the puppies into the house and sat them in front of the warm fire.

Roger gave them plenty to eat and drink and tucked them into a warm bed. He even hung stockings over the end.

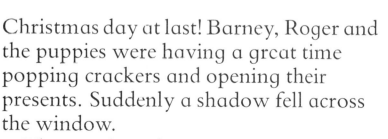

Christmas day at last! Barney, Roger and the puppies were having a great time popping crackers and opening their presents. Suddenly a shadow fell across the window.

The Prophet of Doom had come for his special surprise.

"Quickly," whispered Barney to the puppies,
"hop into this box." And by the time
Roger opened the door to Mr Prophet,
the box was ready with a floppy
red bow. Barney handed over the
present. Out sprang the little
dalmatian puppies.
"Surprise!" they squealed.
"Happy Christmas to you,
lovely old cuddly."

Mr Prophet just fell back into an armchair, his jaw wide open. He got out his box of tissues and blew his nose most loudly . . . . or did he wipe away a tear?

Then he leaned over to the puppies and said, "Thank you, for making an old dog happy."
  The puppies gave him a huge Christmas hug. "Thank you for finding us," they said.

"It's a funny old world," sniffed Mr Prophet. "Things always change – you're lost and you're found!"

"That's settled then," said Barney, springing up. He pointed to one puppy, "you're Lost," he said, and he turned to the other, "and you're Found."

And that's how the puppies got their names and how Mr Prophet got his Christmas smile.